# Oh say can you say?

By
**Dr. Seuss**

# 說話繞口令

文・圖　蘇斯博士
譯　曾陽晴

## 說話繞口令

蘇斯博士小孩學讀書全集8

發行／1992 年 12 月 25 日初版 1 刷　　2003 年 4 月 21 日初版 5 刷

著／蘇斯博士

譯／曾陽晴

責任編輯／郝廣才　張玲玲　劉思源

美術編輯／李純真　郭倖惠　陳素芳

發行人／王榮文　　出版發行／遠流出版事業股份有限公司　　台北市汀州路3段184號7樓之5

行政院新聞局局版臺業字第1295號　　郵撥／0189456-1　　電話／(02)2365-3707　　傳真／(02)2365-7979

著作權顧問／蕭雄淋律師　　法律顧問／王秀哲律師・董安丹律師

印製／鴻柏印刷事業股份有限公司

YL*ib* 遠流博識網 http://www.ylib.com　　E-mail:ylib@ylib.com

ISBN 957-32-1426-1

NT＄185

Said a book-reading parrot named Hooey,
"The words in this book are all phooey.
When you say them, your lips
will make slips and back flips
and your tongue may end up in Saint Looey!"

念ㄋㄧㄢˋ書ㄕㄨ鸚ㄧㄥ鵡ㄨˇ叫ㄐㄧㄠˋ胡ㄏㄨˊ語ㄩˇ，

牠ㄊㄚ說ㄕㄨㄛ：「這ㄓㄜˋ本ㄅㄣˇ書ㄕㄨ好ㄏㄠˇ驢ㄌㄩˊ，

嘴ㄗㄨㄟˇ唇ㄔㄨㄣˊ念ㄋㄧㄢˋ來ㄌㄞˊ好ㄏㄠˇ容ㄖㄨㄥˊ易ㄧˋ

滑ㄏㄨㄚˊ不ㄅㄨˋ溜ㄌㄧㄡ丟ㄉㄧㄡ、顛ㄉㄧㄢ三ㄙㄢ倒ㄉㄠˋ四ㄙˋ，

念ㄋㄧㄢˋ完ㄨㄢˊ舌ㄕㄜˊ頭ㄊㄡˊ跑ㄆㄠˇ到ㄉㄠˋ聖ㄕㄥˋ路ㄌㄨˋ易ㄧˋ！」

新鮮的 FRESH    更新鮮的 FRESHER    最新鮮的 FRESHEST

Do you like fresh fish?
It's just fine at Finney's Diner.
Finney also has some fresher fish
that's fresher and much finer.
But his best fish is his freshest fish
and Finney says with pride,
"The finest fish at Finney's
is my freshest fish, French-fried!"

你喜歡吃新鮮的魚嗎？
在好廚子餐館裡這條魚算還好。
好廚子還有更新鮮的魚，
那條魚更新鮮而且更好。
不過， 他最好的魚是那條最新鮮的魚，
好廚子很驕傲的說道：
「 這條最新鮮的魚在我的好廚子餐館裡，
是最新鮮的一條魚， 炸得很美妙！」

SO...
don't order the fresh
or the fresher fish.
At Finney's, if you're wise,
you'll say,
"Fetch me the finest
French-fried freshest
fish that Finney fries!"

所以……

別點那條新鮮的魚

或是那條更新鮮的魚。

到好廚子餐館用餐， 如果你夠內行，

你就會指名說：

「 我點的是最好的、

炸得最脆的、 最新鮮的、

由好廚子親自炸的那條魚！」

# Dinn's Shin

老丁的脛骨

We have a dinosaur named Dinn.
Dinn's thin. Dinn doesn't have much skin.
And the bones fall out
of his left front shin.

我們有一隻恐龍叫老丁。
老丁瘦巴巴，老丁沒有多少皮膚。
還有根骨頭掉出他左前腳的脛骨。

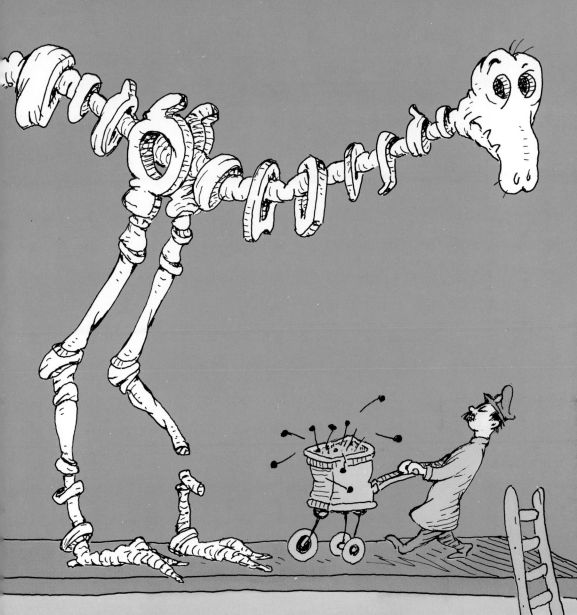

Then we have to call in Pinner Blinn,
who comes with his handy shin-pin bin
and with a thin Blinn shinbone pin,
Blinn pins Dinn's shinbones right back in.

所以我們找來了一位釘骨師叫包靈，
他推著裝了脛骨釘的手推車好神氣！
只用一支細細的包靈脛骨釘，
就把老丁的脛骨釘回去。

Bed Spreaders spread spreads on beds.
Bread Spreaders spread butters on breads.
And that Bed Spreader better
watch out how he's spreading...

鋪床鋪的老王鋪了床鋪在床上。
抹麵包奶油的老張抹了奶油在麵包上。
鋪床鋪的老王最好是
注意他鋪床鋪的方式……

or that Bread Spreader's
sure going to butter his bedding.
要ㄠ不ㄠ然ㄖ抹ㄇ麵ㄇ包ㄅ奶ㄋ油ㄡ的ㄉ老ㄌ張ㄓ
一ㄧ定ㄉ會ㄏ把ㄅ奶ㄋ油ㄡ抹ㄇ上ㄕ他ㄊ的ㄉ床ㄔ。

# Ape Cakes
# Grape Cakes

猩猩蛋糕
葡萄蛋糕

As he gobbled the cakes on his plate,
the greedy ape said as he ate,
"The greener green grapes are,
the keener keen apes are
to gobble green grape cakes.
They're GREAT！"

大ㄉㄚ口ㄎㄡ大ㄉㄚ口ㄎㄡ吃ㄔ盤ㄆㄢ子ㄗˇ裡ㄌㄧˇ的ㄉㄜ蛋ㄉㄢ糕ㄍㄠ
貪ㄊㄢ心ㄒㄧㄣ的ㄉㄜ猩ㄒㄧㄥ猩ㄒㄧㄥ邊ㄅㄧㄢ吃ㄔ邊ㄅㄧㄢ説ㄕㄨㄛ道ㄉㄠˋ：
「綠ㄌㄩˋ色ㄙㄜˋ的ㄉㄜ葡ㄆㄨˊ萄ㄊㄠˊ越ㄩㄝˋ綠ㄌㄩˋ越ㄩㄝˋ妙ㄇㄧㄠˋ
精ㄐㄧㄥ明ㄇㄧㄥ的ㄉㄜ猩ㄒㄧㄥ猩ㄒㄧㄥ心ㄒㄧㄣ裡ㄌㄧˇ就ㄐㄧㄡˋ越ㄩㄝˋ想ㄒㄧㄤˇ要ㄧㄠˋ，
想ㄒㄧㄤˇ要ㄧㄠˋ大ㄉㄚ口ㄎㄡ大ㄉㄚ口ㄎㄡ吃ㄔ綠ㄌㄩˋ色ㄙㄜˋ的ㄉㄜ葡ㄆㄨˊ萄ㄊㄠˊ蛋ㄉㄢ糕ㄍㄠ。
眞ㄓㄣ是ㄕˋ好ㄏㄠˇ吃ㄔ得ㄉㄜ不ㄅㄨˋ得ㄉㄜ了ㄌㄧㄠˇ！」

Are you having trouble
in saying this stuff?
It's really quite easy for me.
I just look in my mirror
and see what I say,
and then I just say what I see.

你有沒有什麼問題，
念出看到的這些東西？
我念起來可真是容易。
我只要注視手裡的鏡子，
看看我念些什麼東西，
不就等於念出了我看到的東西。

# Now let's talk about MONEY!

## 我們來討論一下錢的問題！

You should leave your Grox home when you travel by air.
If you take him along, they charge double the fare.
And your Grox must be packed and locked up in a Grox Box,
which costs much, much more than a little old fox box.
So it's heaps a lot cheaper to fly with your foxes
than waste all that money on boxes for Groxes.

你應該把你的狗葛洛絲留在家裡

因為你旅行是搭飛機。

如果你帶牠一起飛， 收費可是要雙倍。

而且你的葛洛絲， 一定鎖在葛洛絲專用的狗箱，

狗箱非常非常的昂貴

比老式裝狐狸用的小箱子貴幾百倍。

所以有個方法可以便宜幾百倍

就是帶著你的狐狸一起飛，

而不是浪費金錢一大堆

只為了帶葛洛絲狗箱

一起天上飛。

## And, what do you think costs more?...
## A Simple Thimble
### or
## a Single Shingle?

想想看， 哪一個要比較多錢？ ……
一個簡單的手指套
還是一塊小木片？

## A simple thimble <u>could</u> cost less
## than a single shingle would, I guess.
## So I think that the single shingle <u>should</u>
## cost more than the simple thimble would.

一個簡單的手指套看起來
比一塊小木片便宜， 我猜。
所以我想一塊小木片應該
比一個簡單的手指套昂貴才不奇怪。

If you like to eat potato chips
and chew pork chops on clipper ships,
I suggest that you chew
a few chips and a chop
at Skipper Zipp's Clipper Ship Chip Chop Shop.

如果你想上快艇帆船
吃頓洋芋片和豬排大餐，
我建議你細嚼慢嚥
幾片洋芋片和一客豬排餐，
就在雞婆老船長的快艇帆船
裡面的洋芋豬排餐館。

And if your tongue
is getting queasy,
don't give up.
The next one's EASY!

如果你的舌頭
打了結，　好生氣，
千萬別放棄。
因為下一篇很容易！

There are so many things that you really should know.
And that's why I'm bothering telling you so.
You should know the first names of the Fuddnuddler Brothers
who like to pile each on the heads of the others.
If you start at the top, there are Bipper and Bud
and Skipper and Jipper and Jeffrey and Jud,
Horatio, Horace and Hendrix and Hud,
and then come Dinwoodie and Dinty and Dud,
also Fitzsimmon and Frederick and Fud,
and Slinkey and Stinkey and Stuart and Stud.
And, down at the bottom is poor little Lud.
But if Lud ever sneezes, his name will be MUD.

有好多的事情你真的該知道。
所以我才不厭其煩要說給你知道。
你是該認識一下傅家兄弟打聽一下他們的名字
他們最愛玩疊羅漢的把戲！
如果你從最上面算下去， 就是畢伯和布德
還有史基伯和齊伯以及紀夫瑞和秀德，
賀瑞秀、 賀瑞詩和韓德瑞詩和胡德，
再算下來就是丁伍迪和丁踢和杜德，
還有費滋門和費瑞德瑞克和傅德，
以及史林基和史丁基和史綽特和史德。
最後在最下面的， 就是小可憐陸德。
但是， 如果陸德不小心打了個噴嚏，
他的名字就會是小泥巴馬德。

# QUACK QUACK!

瓜！瓜！

We have two ducks. One blue. One black.
And when our blue duck goes "Quack-quack"
our black duck quickly quack-quacks back.
The quacks Blue quacks make her quite a quacker
but Black is a quicker quacker-backer.

我們有兩隻鴨，一隻藍鴨一隻黑鴨。
當我們的藍鴨叫瓜瓜
我們的黑鴨馬上就瓜瓜回答牠。
藍鴨瓜瓜叫讓牠成為一隻瓜瓜鴨
不過黑鴨卻是一隻馬上瓜瓜回答鴨。

AND... speaking of quacks reminds me of cracks
and stacks and sacks and shacks and Schnacks.
SO...oh say can you say, "I have cracks in my shack,
I have smoke in my stack,
and I think there's a Schnack
in the sack on my back!"

還有……說到瓜瓜

讓我想起了屋頂會開花

以及煙囪和大麻袋

還有小屋子和怪鳥乖乖。

所以……練習念念這段話：

「我的小屋子的屋頂開了花，

屋頂煙囪的煙冒得滿天爬，

還有我想怪鳥乖乖

待在我背上的大麻袋裡

不肯離開！」

# WEST BEAST

西邊的怪獸

Upon an island hard to reach,
the East Beast sits upon his beach.
Upon the west beach sits the West Beast.
Each beach beast thinks he's the best beast.

在一座遙遠的小島上，

東邊的怪獸坐在牠的海灘上。

西邊的海灘上坐著西邊的怪獸。

每一隻海灘怪獸都想自己才是最優秀的怪獸。

# EAST BEAST

## 東邊的怪獸

Which beast is best?... Well, I thought at first
that the East was best and the West was worst.
Then I looked again from the west to the east
and I liked the beast on the east beach least.

哪隻怪獸才最優秀？ ……起先我的意見是
東邊怪獸最優秀， 西邊怪獸最醜陋。
後來， 我又從西邊到東邊再看一遍，
我才發現自己一點也不喜歡東邊的怪獸。

# Pete Pats Pigs

## 皮肚拍豬

Pete Briggs pats pigs.

Briggs pats pink pigs.

Briggs pats big pigs.

(Don't ask me why. It doesn't matter.)

Pete Briggs is a pink pig, big pig patter.

布ㄨˋ皮ㄆˊ肚ㄉㄨˋ先ㄒㄢ生ㄕㄥ拍ㄆㄞ豬ㄓㄨ。

布ㄨˋ先ㄒㄢ生ㄕㄥ拍ㄆㄞ粉ㄈㄣ紅ㄏㄨㄥ色ㄙㄜ的ㄉㄜ豬ㄓㄨ。

布ㄨˋ先ㄒㄢ生ㄕㄥ拍ㄆㄞ大ㄉㄚˋ豬ㄓㄨ。

（別ㄅㄧㄝ問ㄨㄣ我ㄨㄛ爲ㄨㄟ什ㄕˊ麼ㄇㄜ，　這ㄓㄜˋ只ㄓˇ是ㄕˋ小ㄒㄠ事ㄕˋ，　不ㄅㄨˋ必ㄅㄧˋ費ㄈㄟˋ神ㄕㄣˊ。）

布ㄨˋ皮ㄆˊ肚ㄉㄨˋ先ㄒㄢ生ㄕㄥ是ㄕˋ一ㄧ個ㄍㄜ喜ㄒㄧˇ歡ㄏㄨㄢ拍ㄆㄞ粉ㄈㄣ紅ㄏㄨㄥ豬ㄓㄨ、　大ㄉㄚˋ豬ㄓㄨ的ㄉㄜ人ㄖㄣˊ。

Pete Briggs pats his big pink pigs all day.
(Don't ask me why. I cannot say.)
Then Pete puts his patted pigs away
in his Pete Briggs' Pink Pigs Big Pigs Pigpen.

布皮肚先生一整天都在拍他的粉紅色大豬。

（別問我為什麼，原因我說不出。）

然後布皮肚把他拍過的豬

關進布皮肚先生的粉紅豬大豬圈裡頭。

傅力子食物

Fritz needs Fred and Fred needs Fritz.
Fritz feeds Fred and Fred feeds Fritz.
Fred feeds Fritz with ritzy Fred food.
Fritz feeds Fred with ritzy Fritz food.
And Fritz, when fed, has often said,
"I'm a Fred-fed Fritz.
Fred's a Fritz-fed Fred."

傅力子需要傅雷德，傅雷德需要傅力子。
傅力子餵傅雷德，傅雷德餵傅力子。
傅雷德用高級的傅雷德食品餵傅力子。
傅力子用高級的傅力子食品餵傅雷德。
傅力子在吃東西時，通常會表示：
「我是傅雷德餵養的小狗傅力子，
傅雷德是傅力子餵養的傅雷德。」

# How to tell a Klotz from a Glotz

## 如何分辨克羅慈和哥羅慈

Well, the Glotz, you will notice, has lots of black spots.
The Klotz is quite different with lots of black dots.
But the big problem is that the spots on a Glotz
are about the same size as the dots on a Klotz.
So you first have to spot who the one with the dots is.
Then it's easy to tell who the Klotz or the Glotz is.

你會注意到哥羅慈身上

有很多黑斑點。

克羅慈就大不一樣

牠有很多黑圓點。

不過有個問題不簡單：

哥羅慈身上的黑斑點

居然大小和形狀

都和克羅慈身上的黑圓點一模一樣。

所以你先得說對

身上有圓點的是誰。

這樣就很容易分出

誰是克羅慈，　誰是哥羅慈。

# What would you rather be when you Grow Up?

你長大後想當什麼？

A cop in a cop's cap?
Or a cupcake cook
in a cupcake cook's cap?
Or a fat flapjack flapper
in a flat flapped-jack cap?

當警察，戴警帽？
還是當廚師，烤蛋糕，
戴頂蛋糕廚師帽？
或是當一個胖胖的煎餅人，
戴頂扁扁的煎餅帽？

OR...
if you think
you don't like cops' caps,
flapjack flappers'
or cupcake cooks' caps,
maybe you're one
of those choosy chaps
who likes kooky captains' caps
perhaps.

或者是……
如果你想到
你不喜歡警帽、
煎餅人的煎餅帽、
或是蛋糕廚師帽，
也許你可以當
老愛挑剔的少年郎，
喜歡奇怪的軍官帽，
這也很好。

# More about Blinn

## 包靈先生

Well, when Blinn comes home tired
from his work pinning shins,
the happiest hour of old Blinn's day begins.
Mr. Blinn is the father of musical twins
who, tucking twin instruments under twin chins,
lull their daddy to sleep with twin Blinn violins.

包靈釘好恐龍的脛骨

回到了家，累得一塌糊塗，

不過老包靈一天中最舒服的時刻才剛啓幕……

包靈先生是一對雙胞胎兄弟的爸爸，

他倆把兩隻樂器夾在兩個下巴下面拉，

拉著兩隻包靈小提琴帶領爸爸進入夢鄉。

AND...oh say can you say,
"Far away in Berlin
a musical urchin named Gretchen von Schwinn
has a blue-footed, true-footed,
trick-fingered, slick-fingered,
six-fingered, six-stringed tin Schwinn mandolin."

還有……練習念念下面這段話：

「　在那遙遠的柏林，

有位來自樹蔭家族的音樂小頑童名叫萬瑞珍，

她有隻奇怪的琴：　有雙藍色的腳，　真正的腳，

有會變魔術的手指頭，　靈巧滑溜的手指頭，

有六隻手指頭、　六條琴弦、

用錫做的樹蔭曼陀林琴。」

# Rope Soap 繩子肥皂
# Hoop Soap 呼拉圈肥皂

If you hope
to wash soup off a rope,
simply scrub it with SKROPE!
## Skrope is so strong that no rope is too lon

如果你希望

洗掉繩子上面的湯，

只要用司克羅普刷刷就很棒！

而且再長的繩子也不夠看，

因為司克羅普效力真正強！

But if you should wish to wash
soup off a hoop, I suggest that it's best
to let your whole silly souped-up hoop soak
in Soapy Cooper's Super Soup-Off-Hoops Soak Suds.

不ㄅㄨˋ過ㄍㄨㄛˋ，　如ㄖㄨˊ果ㄍㄨㄛˇ你ㄋㄧˇ希ㄒㄧ望ㄨㄤˋ洗ㄒㄧˇ掉ㄉㄧㄠˋ
呼ㄏㄨ拉ㄌㄚ圈ㄑㄩㄢ上ㄕㄤˋ的ㄉㄜ˙湯ㄊㄤ，　我ㄨㄛˇ建ㄐㄧㄢˋ議ㄧˋ你ㄋㄧˇ最ㄗㄨㄟˋ好ㄏㄠˇ
把ㄅㄚˇ你ㄋㄧˇ那ㄋㄚˋ個ㄍㄜˋ沾ㄓㄢ了ㄌㄜ˙湯ㄊㄤ的ㄉㄜ˙笨ㄅㄣˋ呼ㄏㄨ拉ㄌㄚ圈ㄑㄩㄢ整ㄓㄥˇ個ㄍㄜˋ浸ㄐㄧㄣˋ到ㄉㄠˋ
裝ㄓㄨㄤ滿ㄇㄢˇ超ㄔㄠ級ㄐㄧˊ呼ㄏㄨ拉ㄌㄚ圈ㄑㄩㄢ湯ㄊㄤ汁ㄓ洗ㄒㄧˇ潔ㄐㄧㄝˊ去ㄑㄩˋ污ㄨ肥ㄈㄟˊ皂ㄗㄠˋ水ㄕㄨㄟˇ
的ㄉㄜ˙肥ㄈㄟˊ皂ㄗㄠˋ桶ㄊㄨㄥˇ裡ㄌㄧˇ才ㄘㄞˊ可ㄎㄜˇ靠ㄎㄠˋ。

One year we had a Christmas brunch
with Merry Christmas Mush to munch.
But I don't think you'd care for such.
We didn't like to munch mush much.

有ㄧㄡˇ一ㄧˋ年ㄋㄧㄢˊ，　我ㄨㄛˇ們ㄇㄣˊ吃ㄔ聖ㄕㄥˋ誕ㄉㄢˋ節ㄐㄧㄝˊ特ㄊㄜˋ餐ㄘㄢ
喝ㄏㄜ了ㄌㄜ一ㄧˋ頓ㄉㄨㄣˋ聖ㄕㄥˋ誕ㄉㄢˋ快ㄎㄨㄞˋ樂ㄌㄜˋ稀ㄒㄧ飯ㄈㄢˋ。
不ㄅㄨˋ過ㄍㄨㄛˋ我ㄨㄛˇ想ㄒㄧㄤˇ我ㄨㄛˇ們ㄇㄣˊ吃ㄔ什ㄕㄜˊ麼ㄇㄜ你ㄋㄧˇ才ㄘㄞˊ不ㄅㄨˋ管ㄍㄨㄢˇ。
而ㄦˊ且ㄑㄧㄝˇ我ㄨㄛˇ們ㄇㄣˊ自ㄗˋ己ㄐㄧˇ也ㄧㄝˇ不ㄅㄨˋ太ㄊㄞˋ喜ㄒㄧˇ歡ㄏㄨㄢ聖ㄕㄥˋ誕ㄉㄢˋ稀ㄒㄧ飯ㄈㄢˋ。

# And, speaking of Christmas...
## 說到了聖誕節⋯

Here are
some Great Gifts
to give to your daddy!

在這裡
有一些很棒的禮
要送給你的爹地！

If your daddy's name is Jim
and if Jim swims and if Jim's slim,
the perfect Christmas gift for him
is a set of Slim Jim Swim Fins.

如果你爹地的名字是吉姆，

如果吉姆會游泳， 如果吉姆是個瘦排骨，

那麼， 送他的最好聖誕禮物

就是一套瘦子吉姆專用的蛙鞋和泳褲。

But if your daddy's name is Dwight
and he likes to look at birds at night,
the gift for Dwight that might be right
is a Bright Dwight Bird-Flight
Night-Sight Light.

可是，如果你爹地的名字是杜威
而且他喜歡在晚上看鳥飛，
那麼你最好送給杜威
一個明亮的杜威專用飛鳥
夜視照明燈，讓他晚上看鳥飛。

# But Never Give Your Daddy a Walrus

不過，千萬別送你爹地一隻海象

A walrus with whiskers is not a good pet.
And a walrus which whispers is worse even yet.
When a walrus lisps whispers
through tough rough wet whiskers,
your poor daddy's ear
will get blispers and bliskers.

有鬍鬚的海象做寵物養並不好。
要是這隻海象還喜歡在人耳邊
低聲細語，那就更加糟糕。
海象把牠嘰哩咕嚕的低聲細語，
從又硬又粗的鬍鬚之間傾訴出去，
你可憐爹地的耳朵就會倒大霉，
劈哩拍啦沾得都是口水。

And that's almost enough
of such stuff for one day.
One more and you're finished.
*Oh say can you say?......*

眞是讓人慘兮兮，
一天裡面念這麼多東西。
快念完了，只剩下最後一篇。
來，再念念看……

"The storm starts
when the drops start dropping.
When the drops stop dropping
then the storm starts stopping."

「暴風雨開始
是從雨滴開始滴下時。
當雨滴停止滴下時，
暴風雨也就開始停止。」